SCALES OF HONESTY

AN EGYPTIAN EMPIRE STORY

LAURA GREENWOOD

BLURB

Being a priestess for the goddess of truth and justice is not for the faint-hearted.

Taia always thought she and fellow Ma'at Blessed priest, Metjen, were inseparable. When he starts avoiding her, she questions whether their bond is as strong as she thought it was.

A big festival to celebrate the temples in London comes with a test of Taia's devotion and the goddess of truth and justice is not one to displease.

Can Taia and Metjen figure out what's causing the problems between them before they risk losing the blessing of their goddess?

-

Scales Of Honesty is a standalone companion story to The Apprentice Of Anubis series, an urban fantasy set in an alternative version of London where the Egyptian Empire never fell. Scales Of Honesty can be read as a standalone.

The events take place during the events of Festival Of The Blessed.

If you love Egyptian mythology, alternative versions of the modern day, temple politics, and slow-burn workplace romance, then start the Apprentice Of Anubis series today with Apprentice Of The Dead.

A BRIEF NOTE

The Apprentice Of Anubis series is set in an alternative universe where the Egyptian Empire never fell and replaced the Roman Empire. The split in the timeline happened after the Ptolemaic dynasty and the final Cleopatra's infamous reign. Instead of Egypt falling into the hands of the Romans, they fought back and gained control of the budding Roman Empire. All religions still exist in the world, but many have been absorbed into the Egyptian religion (this was common practice during their ancient history, so is something I adopted into the series).

For the purposes of this series, the Egyptian Empire spans much of Africa and Europe, as well as some of the Middle East.

I made the decision to keep a lot of the words

and systems we use today (including place names like London and the River Thames) to make the reading experience as smooth as possible. If this was the real progression of events, those things would likely have been named differently.

Things I have kept are the Ancient Egyptian concept of a week (10 days, including a 2 day "weekend"), month (3 weeks), season (4 months) and year (3 seasons plus 5 feast days). The currency they're using is debens (derived from the Ancient Egyptian word for bread - something workers were often paid in). Names have also been influenced by Ancient Egyptian history.

ONE

I FIDGET with my dress and resist the urge to straighten my headdress, feeling incredibly underdressed compared to most of the other Blessed in the room. But there's nothing I can do about it. These are the only jewels I have, which means they're what I have to wear for formal occasions.

I just wish it wasn't the case.

"What's wrong, Taia?" a familiar voice asks.

I turn to find my Blessed partner standing beside me and smile at him. Why does he have to look so good in his formal wear? I know his jewels aren't much better than mine, but the confidence with which he wears them makes all the difference.

"Nothing," I respond.

Metjen snorts in disbelief. "I might not be able to

tell when someone's telling me the truth, but I know when you're lying. What's up?"

I sigh. "I feel out of place," I admit. "And being here makes me nervous."

"Why? It's not our Day of Choosing, all we have to do is assist the older Ma'at Blessed with their jobs."

"I know." It still doesn't help me.

"Your jewels?" he guesses.

I nod.

"I think you look beautiful in them."

My Blessed sense tingles within me the same way it does when someone is telling me the truth. But it's not the only response I have to the words, and my heart skips a beat at them, and the possible implications of him saying them.

I push the thought to the side. I know these feelings are probably just because we spend so much time together. I don't want to be one of the Blessed pairs who end up together by default even if my heart currently likes the sound of the idea.

It's just a phase, which is something I need to remember.

"I guess I'm a bit worried about the Scales Test," I admit, though mostly as a diversion so he doesn't catch on to the real thoughts in my head.

"Isn't that months away?"

I nod. "But we've never done a Festival of the Blessed before, I guess I'm worried about how it's going to go."

"We'll be fine, Taia."

My Blessed sense tingles. It might not be *the* truth, but it's his truth. And I suppose that's the most important thing considering one of his roles as a Blessed is to keep me and my motivations in check. Of course the other is to determine a fair punishment, but that's not exactly something relevant to the two of us.

"Is everyone ready?" Benemba calls from the front of the room.

I turn to face her, a serene smile in place before I do. I know that this is all about appearances.

"Okay, follow me." She gestures for us to leave the room.

"You've got this," Metjen says, brushing his hand against my lower back as he does.

A shiver threatens to run down my spine, but I manage to stop it before it does. I'm surprised that he hasn't worked out how I'm feeling yet, but perhaps that's just because he can't sense when someone's lying the same way I can.

I ignore all of my personal issues and head towards the front of the room where a row of golden scales sit waiting for us. I pick one of them up, surprised by how heavy they are. The Blessed priestess holding them on my Day of Choosing didn't look as if they were, but maybe I'm remembering wrong. It is the day that changed my life. I wanted to work for Ma'at's temple even then, but I had no idea the goddess would choose me to be one of her Blessed priests.

I shift the scales in my hands and fall into line behind Benemba. I know it's an honour that she picked me to walk beside her with the scales, and that she's doing it to reward me for the work I did with the elections at the Temple of Anubis, but I can't help feeling unworthy when I'm beside her.

Despite that, I know that I'm here and that I need to do my duty.

Silence follows us all as we step out of the room and into the large courtyard where the eighteen-year-olds wait for the gods to make their choices and reveal the Blessed to them. There are gaps in most of the lines, presumably where the sacred animals of the other gods have claimed their new masters.

I never felt jealousy over the fact that the other Blessed got sacred animals to be their companions, not until I met Ani from the Temple of Anubis and her adorable jackal. But that's not what I wanted for myself. *This* is what I wanted. To serve Ma'at and make sure that justice and balance were a part of the world.

Benemba stops at the first row of potential priests and priestesses. I stop behind her along with Metjen, while the other Blessed make their way through the hall and into their positions. I know from experience just how imposing this looks from the other side.

The silence is deafening, with the shuffle of hundreds of bodies in a relatively small space, and the creak of the scales as they dip up and down. The weight is frustrating and I can already feel the burn of carrying them in my shoulders. I'm going to pay for this honour in the morning.

Benemba starts making her way down the line, stopping in front of each person and looking at the scales to see if they balance. It isn't until we're six people deep that they start to do as much. I watch in awe as they flatten, stopping every movement. I hold my breath and wait to see if a feather appears to signal that they're Blessed, or if the guy in front of us is just to be a standard priest.

Nothing happens, and despite the fact it's not for me, I feel a little disappointed.

"Welcome to the Temple of Ma'at," Benemba says loudly enough for most people in our immediate vicinity to hear. "Blessed Priest Metjen will lead you to where you'll be briefed." She gestures for the new apprentice to follow Metjen, who smiles at him and ushers him to the end of the line, pointing him towards one of the open doorways. I don't know what will happen once he's through there, on my own Day of Choosing, I went through the Blessed door.

As soon as Metjen rejoins us, Benemba begins the ritual all over again, sending two more people through the door. But no Blessed. I hope the others are getting on better. Ma'at is known for picking numerous Blessed every year.

We come to the end of the line where a girl nervously fiddling with her hair is standing and waiting. I instantly feel the shift in the scales and they balance perfectly. A feather appears on the right-hand side of the scale. It hangs steady, glittering in the light and leaving no doubt about what it means.

Her eyes widen, much like I imagine mine did on this day three years ago. There's nothing like realising that a goddess has chosen you to serve her.

"Welcome to the Temple of Ma'at, Blessed Apprentice," Benemba says.

"I'm Blessed?" the girl asks, looking between me and Benemba.

I smile and give her what I hope is a reassuring nod.

"Please follow Blessed Priest Metjen, he will instruct you on where to go next," Benemba says, barely even registering the surprise of the girl whose life has just changed.

Seeing it happen in front of me makes the burn in my shoulders disappear and makes my Blessed sense tingle even stronger than normal.

I feel connected to my goddess, and that's always something I'm going to welcome with open arms.

TWO

TABLES CROWD the street outside the Temple of Ma'at and chatter rises through the air as the party to open the Festival of the Blessed gets underway. It barely seems like yesterday that the Day of Choosing was here, and yet it's already been months. I guess life at the temple never really stops.

I smile at several of the priests I know from around the table and find a spot at the table with the priests and priestesses who started as apprentices at the same time as I did. In the two years since we were ordained, our paths have drifted away from one another, but we always seem to end up back at the same table when festivals come around. It's nice to have people I recognise around, even if I feel like I barely know them anymore.

"Taia!" Heqet says, smiling widely at me.

"Hey," I respond to her as I take a seat.

"It's good to see you, it's been what? Three months."

"Something like that." It might even be more.

"I heard that you and Metjen were assigned to the elections at the Temple of Anubis," Heqet says, grabbing a slice of bread from the platter in the middle of the table.

"We were."

She sighs. "Ah, to be Blessed. That must have been really interesting."

I think back over the month we spent there. "I guess it was."

"And such an honour. What's their Blessed like? They have one, right?" She's so excited about things that have become mundane to me. I'm not even fully sure how to deal with it.

"They do," I confirm, grabbing an apple and cutting it into slices. "She's nice."

"It must be so cool to be Blessed," she says wistfully.

"Yeah." Apart from the fact that I don't seem to have any proper friendships any more, most people consider me a pariah because they're always worried about my Blessed sense. It's weird because it wouldn't be a problem if people were just honest with me. I can't tell what secrets people are hiding, only when they're outright lying to my face.

And I'm not in the habit of asking questions I don't want the answers to.

"Where's Metjen?" Heqet asks, drawing me out of my thoughts.

"Hmm, I'm not sure actually." I look around for him, finally spotting him talking with one of our Blessed mentors. I wave and he returns the gesture, making my heart flutter.

"It must be crazy living with him," Heqet says. "I always wanted to ask him on a date."

"You did?" My voice comes out a little squeaky, and I hope that she doesn't notice and think badly of me for it.

"Of course. Have you seen him?" She gives a little dreamy sigh that I'm not entirely sure I disagree with, though I hate that's

"I live with him," I point out, though I'm not sure if there's any real reason to draw attention to that.

"I know. Is he as hot as he looks?" she asks.

I blink a few times and look over to where my Blessed partner is standing and try not to think about what he looks like shirtless. Or be disappointed that he's opted for a tunic as his formal wear and not just a kilt like some of the other guys around us. "I don't know, I haven't spent much time looking," I lie, the words feeling ashen on my tongue as if I'm disobeying my goddess just by saying them.

Which I know isn't true. She's not paying any attention to my dating life or lack thereof. Maybe it would be different if I was serving one of the fertility goddesses, but that's not the case here.

"Is he seeing anyone now?" Heqet asks.

"I don't know." I try to squash down the jealousy rearing its head up inside me.

"Ah, that's a shame. What about you? Are you seeing anyone?"

"Oh, no." Mostly because it's difficult to date when I live with another guy. And that's only the second reason that people don't want to date me.

Or be my friend.

"I have a friend I can set you up with," Heqet offers. "You'd like him. He's the apprentice to a coffin-maker, so not in the priesthood, but I think you'll like him."

"Oh, erm, are you sure?" I'm a little taken aback by the suggestion and I'm not really sure what to do with it.

She nods. "I think you'll get on really well. Want me to set it up?"

I glance over to where Metjen is standing, trying

to find a reason to say no that isn't him. But I come up with nothing.

"Sure, that'd be good," I say, mostly because I can't think of a way to say no without potentially insulting her.

"Great. I'll let you know what he says." She smiles at me. "I want to hear all about it."

My Blessed sense wavers, telling me that her response is somewhere between a truth and a lie. She's probably just thinking about the reality of when our paths will cross again. I like Heqet, and as far as I can tell, she likes me too, but I'm Blessed and she's not. That always puts some kind of barrier between us.

"I look forward to it," I respond.

Metjen waves me over to him. If only he could have rescued me *before* I agreed to a date.

"You're lucky, Taia," Heqet says. "Tell him hi from me."

"I will." I get to my feet and wave goodbye to the other priests and priestesses, though none of them are really paying any attention to me.

I ignore the crowded tables and only stop when I'm by my Blessed partner.

"You looked like you could use rescuing," Metjen says.

"A little too late, I think. Heqet wants to set us up with people." I grimace at the mere thought of it.

He groans. "Oh no. Tell me who?"

"A coffin-maker's apprentice for me, and I think her for you. Or that's what she was hinting at."

"Eurgh. Not again." There's a definite note of frustration in his voice.

I raise an eyebrow and try to ignore the churning in my stomach. "Again?"

"She tried to instigate something a few times when we were apprentices."

"I didn't realise."

Metjen shrugs. "Why should you? I turned her down, it was no big deal." He grabs two glasses of wine from a passing tray and holds one out to me.

I take it from him, my fingers brushing against his as I take it, sending a tingle across my skin that I choose to ignore.

"I think she'd go there still, if you've changed your mind," I say, all while hoping that he hasn't.

He sighs. "It's hard. She's nice, but you know when you just don't feel something for someone?"

"Mmhmm."

"I guess I just don't feel that *thing*, you know? Like I wouldn't want to spend the rest of my life with her. Would you?" he asks.

"Spend the rest of my life with Heqet? She's not really my type."

"You've dated so little that I don't know what your type is," Metjen quips.

"What's anyone's type? Sweet, hardworking, honest..." *You.*

I startle at the thought and banish it to the furthest depths of my mind. I can't think like that. The only reason I'm thinking it is because so many of the Blessed pairs end up together. That's all this is. Inevitability.

"Maybe I should just skip all of the dating and decide I'm spending the rest of my life with you," Metjen muses.

"What?" I squeak.

"Well we're stuck together, right? Unless one of us has our blessing removed," he jokes, though it's almost as if I can hear something serious in his voice, but I know it's probably my imagination.

"Oh, right. That. Yep, I guess we're stuck with each other."

And right now, I'm not entirely sure that sounds like a good thing, especially if I can't get my feelings into check.

THREE

I LOOK up at the huge statues of Ma'at which dominate the entrance to the temple. I know some people find them imposing, even those who work here themselves, but I find them comforting. There's something about the slight smile on the goddess' lips, and the look in her eyes that dares people to try lying to her, that I find reassuring. I always have done. This is the gaze that keeps the world in check, that chooses truth and justice over personal gain.

I can't remember when I started to admire Ma'at so much, but the goddess has been my favourite since I was little. Maybe that's not the most balanced choice for me to make, but I've never been able to help it.

I make my way up the steps and enter the temple, ignoring the temple servants who are going about their tasks for the day, as well as the few priests who are probably going about personal business at this time in the evening.

I suppose I'm doing the same.

The public parts of the temple give way to the living quarters and the corridors grow smaller, but no less grandly decorated. Ma'at's carved face is everywhere, along with the scales and feathers that denote her power. Whoever designed the London Temple of Ma'at wanted everyone to remember precisely where they were.

I don't mind so much, but I can see why people find it imposing to be here. Especially if they have something to hide.

Much like the coffin-making apprentice Heqet set me up with. I don't think the date could have gone worse. He was charming, sure, but there was something off about him. No doubt it was exactly the same as always. People find me intimidating not because of me, but because of my ability to sense when they're lying and everything I stand for.

I love serving my goddess, it's everything I've ever wanted, but it's lonely. And with very little time spent with the other Blessed my own age, it wasn't like I'd been able to replace the friends I'd lost.

I reach the door to the apartment I share with Metjen and some of the thoughts disappear. At least there's one person I can always rely on. Whether it's to talk about a bad date where someone's been weird again, or just talking about the weather, he's always there.

Maybe that's why Ma'at really blesses in pairs. It's not about keeping one another in check and maintaining the balance, it's about the loneliness.

I glance at the carved face a few feet over.

Or maybe not. I'm sure Ma'at has plenty of things to worry about above and beyond the way her priests are feeling.

I slip my key into the door and twist it open, stepping inside.

Disappointment floods through me as I realise the lights are dim and that Metjen must have already turned in for the night.

I sigh and shut the door, heading over to the kitchenette so I can make myself a drink. Maybe he'll come out if he hears me wandering around. I certainly hope so, I need to talk to him about the date so I can process what's going through my head.

I pour boiling water into my mug, enjoying the scent of rose petals as it fills the air. There's nothing like my favourite cup of tea to chase away the ghost of bad dates past.

I slip off my bracelets and stick them on the kitchen side. I should put them back in their box so that they stay in the right condition for the next time I need them, but that involves going to my room and I don't want to miss Metjen leaving his.

I glance over in the direction of his closed door, slightly confused about why he's not coming out. He's normally always here when I come back from somewhere on my own, and I'm the same when he does. Sometimes, I find myself making notes of things I want to tell him while I'm still out.

I let out a loud sigh and take the tea bag out of my mug. I give one last longing look at Metjen's room, debating whether I should knock or not, but decide against it. He must be tired if he's not coming out right now, which means that I should save everything for the morning.

I grab my mug and head to my bedroom, shutting the door behind me and hoping that I'm not making a mistake.

I RUB the sleep out of my eyes and take a sip of my morning tea, attempting to hide my confusion about where Metjen is. He's normally sitting eating his breakfast at this time in the morning and getting me to go over our duties for the day.

I look down at my tablet, scanning through the

assignments on my own but not seeing anything of note. Except that our first one is in twenty minutes, and it'll take fifteen for us to get there. I'm going to have to brief Metjen on the way.

It takes another few minutes for his door to open and for him to step out. "Sorry, overslept," he mumbles.

Lie.

A sinking feeling fills me. He's never done that before. I stare at him, not knowing how to respond.

"Let me grab some breakfast, and then we can go," he says, picking up an orange from our fruit basket.

I blink a few times, trying to work out what's happening and still caught up in the fact he lied about oversleeping. Why would he do that?

"Taia? You okay?"

"Yes, sorry. Just thinking, I guess." I force a smile onto my face and get to my feet.

"Great, hopefully about how we're going to deal with our first appointment of the day. What is it again?"

I glance down at my tablet, though I don't really need to. "We need to make a judgement about a shopkeeper who is accusing his competitor of slander."

"Ah, not too complicated then." He runs a hand

through his hair, something he only does if he's uncomfortable.

I want to ask what's going on, but I'm terrified of what's going to happen if he lies to me again. I don't know how to deal with it.

"After that, it's our turn to tend to the shrine in front of the temple," I say.

He groans. "I already forgot that we have duties for the Festival of the Blessed to attend to. What else have we got to do?"

"There's the Banquet of the Blessed tomorrow," I read off my list. "There's more shrine duties, the parade, and then the celebratory banquet at the end. Oh, and the Scales Test."

"You're still worrying about that," he says needlessly.

"Aren't you?"

He shrugs, but doesn't say anything.

I sigh. "We should get going or we're going to be late. I don't want to deal with Benemba's wrath if we are." I drain the rest of my tea and grab my tablet, hoping that whatever weirdness is happening between us right now will disappear over the course of the day. I dread to think of the consequences if it doesn't.

FOUR

THE BANQUET HALL is loud and full of Blessed from all over London talking to their friends and in different stages of drunkenness. I swirl my wine around my glass, searching the crowd for Metjen. It's strange to be at an event like this and not spending all my time with him. We normally do everything together, the same way most Ma'at Blessed pairs do.

But that would involve him actually talking to me, and he doesn't seem to be doing that right now.

I sigh and put my glass down. I don't really want to drink it anyway.

Someone clears their throat and I turn, finding a familiar dark-haired priestess and her jackal standing next to me.

"Mind if I sit with you?" she asks.

I don't think I do a good job of hiding my surprise, but I gesture to the free seat next to me. "Hey, Ani, I forgot you'd probably be coming." I should have thought about it. And the fact that as the only Anubis Blessed in the country, she'd be on her own. Unless I count her sacred jackal.

She sits next to me, taking the drink offered to her by one of the servers.

A black fluffy head pops up by me and I smile despite my contemplative mood. "Hey, Matia." I ruffle the fur on the top of the jackal's head and she pushes it into my touch, which I assume to be a good sign. Ani certainly doesn't seem to be acting in a way that at all suggests her jackal is uncomfortable.

"How long have you been here?" she asks me.

"About half an hour. Our High Priestess likes to make sure everyone is on time to the point of early. You probably met her during the audit." Not that I like the idea of reminding Ani about the most stressful time her temple has ever faced. I wasn't there to see the audit first-hand, but I heard enough from the Ma'at Blessed who were to have an idea about what it was like.

"Probably, but we weren't properly introduced. I mostly just kept my head down so no one figured out..." she trails off, no doubt thinking better of revealing that she's the one who brought Ma'at wrath down on the Temple of Anubis. It probably won't matter if she does considering I already know, and there's no one from the Temple of Anubis here. But these things have a way of getting around. No doubt the only reason it isn't common knowledge is that no one really wants to be friends with the Ma'at Blessed.

"How we know each other?" I suggest instead.

"Yes, that."

"Your new High Priest didn't believe us at all." I can't help the amusement that springs to life inside me at the memory of how he'd responded when we'd said that Metjen and Ani's boyfriend were old school friends.

"He knows Nik." Her affectionate smile leaves no doubt about her feelings for him.

"Mmm, that will do it. I'll admit, it's strange to see you without him."

"It happens sometimes," she responds.

My Blessed sense tingles, letting me know that she's telling the truth. Which isn't really a necessary thing for it to work on, but I have no way of switching it off.

"But you'd rather he was here?" I ask curiously.

"I always rather that." Matia goes to sit beside her and Ani starts absentmindedly stroking her in a way that makes it clear just how much time they spend around one another. "Speaking of people we're normally seen with, where's Metjen?"

Ah, I'd kind of hoped she wouldn't notice. "He's avoiding me." The admission slides out before I have a moment to think about whether I really want to tell her.

"How is that possible? Don't you work together?" Her surprise is evident, and pretty much mirrors my own.

"Yep. But anything outside work, and he's just going out of his way to not speak with me. Which is as awkward as you can imagine when we live in the same flat."

"You live together?"

"The Ma'at Blessed flats come with two rooms. If one of you gets married, you can move out of them, or you can move into specially built ones that are designed for two couples." Saying it out loud makes it sound even weirder than it did the first time I learned about it.

"That sounds like kind of a nightmare," Ani says.

"Don't you live with other priests?"

"Well, yes. And I suppose that does include Nik."

"Weird how they expect us to spend all of our

time around the same people and it still go well for work," I mutter.

"I actually don't mind it. I feel like it made the four of us a better team, which was necessary while the audit was going on. At one point I think we were having to deal with eight bodies between the four of us."

"How many do you normally do?" I ask, realising I know next to nothing about that aspect of her job. Whenever I've worked with Ani, it's been in her role as one of the Blessed, not in her job as an embalmer.

"One between two, I think. But I've not spent much time in the standard mortuary under normal circumstances. They've transferred me to the traditional mummification department now."

"Is that good?" I ask.

"It's what I want to do. Aside from all of this." She waves a hand around the room. "I mean, really it's what I want to do despite all of this."

I let out a bemused thought, thinking of my own dashed career plans. "Yeah, I know what you mean."

"What did you want? Before you were Blessed?" She loads her plate with some food, which is probably a good idea. It's going to be good stuff and I shouldn't waste the opportunity to eat it. The canteen staff at the temple like to try some weird combinations on us all.

"I wanted to work in the accounting department of Ma'at's temple," I admit, not seeing the harm in telling her. Who else is going to understand a change of career plans like another Blessed? "Which I know sounds dull, but I think it's really interesting. Having to check that companies and banks have done their taxes right and that their books all add up? That's the dream."

"Can you not do that as a Blessed, I can see how your Blessed sense would be helpful for that?" she asks.

"Eventually. I have to do my turn as a Blessed mentor before I can specialise." Something I'm not looking forward to at all. I can only imagine how difficult I was to deal with as a new Blessed, and I imagine that I'd draw the short straw and get someone even worse.

"Is that how it works? My mentor never told me how he became one." She picks at the food on her plate, not seeming to pay much attention to it beyond that.

"I have no idea for you, but for Ma'at Blessed, everyone takes a turn at being one, normally after five years of being at the temple, so I have another two to go before it's mine."

"That sucks."

"It's just the way it is." I'm sure there are things at her temple that make her feel that way. A lot of what we do as Blessed, and even as priests in general, seems to be steeped in tradition we can't avoid, even if we want to.

"So, what happened with Metjen?" she asks.

"Are you sure you want to know?" It surprises me how willing I am to talk to her about this, but now she's giving me the opportunity, I'm realising that I want to do just that.

"You don't have to tell me if you don't want to, but I'm here to listen if you do."

My Blessed sense tingles and I narrow my eyes at her.

"I'm telling the truth," she says.

"I know, that's what's confusing."

"Ah, right. Forgot about that for a second. Well, there you go. I'm here to listen."

"But why? We barely know each other?" the question slips out without me meaning it to. I like Ani, and we've gotten on well when we've crossed paths, but I wouldn't say that we're exactly friends.

A thoughtful expression crosses Ani's face. "Because I was dreading coming here tonight. It's bad enough that I have to do all the ceremonies and the formal stuff in my own temple, but everyone's used to me being on my own there, so they're not surprised when I work with Nik, or with any of the others, because I have to. But here? It's different. Everyone else has at least one other Blessed from their temple who they know, and they have people who have done the festival before so know exactly what's going to happen. When I came in and saw you, I felt relieved that I at least knew someone. And I guess there have been times where I felt like we could become friends. So...I guess this is me saying *we should be friends*."

I study her intently, trying to make sense of what's happening. "Not one word of that was a lie."

"I know. I don't make a habit of lying, especially not to Ma'at Blessed." Weirdly, she doesn't seem the slightest bit uncomfortable about that, which isn't something I'm used to. Most people feel like they can't have an honest conversation with me *because* I know when they're lying.

"That's fair. For what it's worth, I'd appreciate a friend. People don't often trust Ma'at Blessed." I don't know what makes me admit it. Maybe because I know she's being honest with me, so it only feels fair that I return the favour.

Ani shrugs. "You're just doing your job."

"I'm sure there are plenty of former priests from your temple who would feel differently," I mutter.

"That's why they were fired. If they had no respect for the job that they were doing, then I have no respect for them. I'm not going to pretend the audit was easy, it really wasn't. There were times when I was cursing Ma'at. Everyone was exhausted, we lost a lot of experienced priests, and morale was at an all-time low. But now we have a High Priest who actually cares and a proper chance to actually do the work that we're supposed to. I'm not going to feel bad about that."

"Good to know." Especially as I know she means every word of it.

She takes a drink. "So, Metjen?"

I sigh, knowing that I need to get this off my chest and talk to someone about it or it's just going to eat me up. "I have no idea what happened. Everything was normal and then I went on a date. He's been avoiding me ever since." One of the only three dates I've been on since I became Ma'at Blessed. It wasn't even a good one, and it ruined things.

"Ah." She sounds as if she understands what's going on better than I do.

"What?"

"It kind of sounds like he's jealous." She feeds Matia a piece of chicken from her plate and the jackal chomps down on it happily.

"No," I say firmly, unable to believe that's the cause of all of this.

"Maybe it's not, you know him better than I do. But Nik acted really weird around me while I was going to banquets with Ramesses."

"Ramesses as in..." It's a popular name thanks to the legacy of the Pharaohs who have shared it, but the way she says it makes it sound as if she's talking about *the* Ramesses.

She grimaces. "Yes, that Ramesses."

"I didn't realise."

"I'm surprised, most people I meet seem to know all about it," she responds.

"What was he like?"

"Considering you can tell when I'm lying and he's the prince of the entire empire, I'm going to refrain from answering that."

She chuckles. "That bad?"

"Worse." *True.* "But it's beside the point. What did you tell Metjen about your date?"

"Nothing, we haven't spoken about anything personal since then." And barely anything work-related either.

She lets out a low whistle. "That's not good."

"No. The worst thing is that it was a really bad date. There was nothing wrong with it on the surface. He was nice enough, paid for dinner even though I tried. It was just not right."

"Yeah, I know that feeling. It doesn't help when you secretly have feelings for someone else either."

"I don't secretly have feelings for anyone," I say instantly, trying not to think too much about the way I've been feeling towards Metjen lately.

Ani flashes me a bemused smile. "I was talking about me, but maybe that's something you should think about."

"I don't want to be a cliché."

"What do you mean?" She takes a drink.

"A lot of Ma'at Blessed end up together. I've been wondering if it's because we spend so much time together so we just know each other well, or if it's more of a default. Not many people like us, even fewer trust us. So we just default end up with one another." It doesn't sound like a good way to spend the rest of my life, even if I like spending my time with Metjen.

"I've wondered that about me and Nik before," she says. "That we're only together because of circumstances."

"And?"

"And I realised that it doesn't matter if that's how we got together. I love him, he makes my life better in more ways than I can count, and I don't want to be without him. That's enough reasons to decide that it doesn't matter. If you and Metjen are feeling more than just friendship for each other, then maybe you should listen to that feeling. What's the worst that can happen?"

"I can sense that you believe what you're saying." There aren't many people whose conviction comes through so strongly in my Blessed sense. I suspect Ani is just one of life's honest people. If she doesn't believe it, then she doesn't say it.

"But you're not sure whether it's the truth, or if I'm just believing that it is?"

"Pretty much," I confirm. I know that some of the other Blessed would prefer it if we kept that part of our powers secret, but that was mostly so they could inspire fear in those around them. Personally, I don't like that very much. We're supposed to serve Ma'at, and the truth is part of that, which means that we should be telling it ourselves.

"I guess you just have to decide if it's worth it. There's only one person who can tell you the truth about that."

"Then it's a shame I'm the only person whose truth I can't sense," I mutter. It would certainly make some things easier.

"Mmm, that's a slight drawback."

"Thank you, Ani."

"You're welcome. And I want to know how it goes. You'll message me, right?" There's a hint of hope in her voice, making me believe her request for friendship.

"You'll be the first person I come to for workplace romance advice," I promise, realising that it might actually be true.

"That might not be a good thing," Ani jokes.

"I've seen you and Nik together, you seem like the real thing."

"You can tell that?" she asks hopefully.

"Not with my Blessed sense, just with my eyes. Neither of you are very good at hiding how much you care for one another. It's not a bad thing unless someone wants to use it against you."

She shrugs. "If they do, it says more about them than us."

"Very true." I smile at her, glad she's chosen to spend her banquet with me and not trying to make friends with some of the other Blessed.

I guess I'm not the only one who has found being Blessed to be a bit lonely sometimes. Hopefully, taking her up on her offer of friendship will mean that I can do something about it.

FIVE

I RESIST the urge to bite my nails, hating the fact that the nervous tick from my childhood has returned. But it's been four days and Metjen hasn't said anything personal to me beyond a few arbitrary greetings.

I glance at him without making it obvious that I'm doing it. He's sitting up straight and looking somewhat uncomfortable. Normally, I'd put it down to the fact that Senemba has called us all together for some reason or other, but I don't think it's that at all.

This is about me.

It has to be, or there's no reason for him lying to me about oversleeping. I know it's a small thing, but I can't get it out of my mind. Metjen has *never* lied to me. And more than that, he knows that I can tell when he is. Which means that he told me a lie with the complete understanding that I'd be able to tell.

"All right everyone, listen up," Senemba says, commanding the attention of the room like no one else can. I suppose she's had plenty of practice at dealing with us over the course of our Blessed training. I glance at the corner of the room where her Blessed partner sits looking bored. I don't think she's ever taken part in any of these teaching moments, though I have no idea why that is.

Silence falls over the room. We're used to listening when she speaks, though I've had less to do with her in the past couple of years. But judging from the people in the room, she's called together anyone who has been Blessed for less than five years, which means that everyone knows and trusts that when Senemba speaks, there's something to listen to.

And that can only mean one thing.

"When I did my first Festival of the Blessed, my mentors never told me anything about the Scales Test," she says. "I hated it. So I promised that if I was ever in a position where I could do it differently, then I would do. It wasn't nice to go into it blind."

I almost let out a sigh of relief. I've only heard about the Scales Test in whispers from older Blessed around the temple, nothing about how it actually works or what we're supposed to do.

"Okay, so on the day, you'll be called to the front of the room one pair at a time," Senemba says. "You'll approach the scales. If the feathers remain on both sides and stay balanced, then you remain Blessed. If the feather disappears, it means the Blessed on that side has lost their blessing."

Horror fills me as I realise what that could mean.

"If the scales unbalance, then you are to be discharged from the temple," Senemba continues without giving us any time to respond. "If the side with the feather is heavier, then you are honourably discharged. If the side with the feather is lighter, then you are dishonourably discharged from the temple."

Worry worms its way through me. Somehow the test is even worse than I expected it to be, and I'm not sure how we're going to pass if Metjen isn't speaking with me.

I look at him, but he's doing everything possible to avoid my gaze.

This has to end. Today. I won't let it carry on any longer than it has to.

"Okay, so if you have any questions, my door is open," Senemba says. "You're dismissed."

Chairs scrape and chatter erupts as everyone starts to make their way out of the room while discussing all of the new information. I don't think I've ever heard all of the younger Blessed being so animated at once.

"Do we have anywhere to be?" Metjen asks.

"No, but..."

"Okay. I'll see you later." He gets to his feet and starts to head towards the door before I can even react.

I shake my head and jump to my feet, hurrying after him. "Metjen?"

He doesn't turn around, even when I catch up with him and grab hold of his wrist.

"Not now, Taia."

"Why are you lying?" My voice cracks as I ask him.

Metjen turns around, a confused expression on his handsome face. "I'm...not."

Voices and the shuffle of feet along the floor make it clear that we shouldn't be having this conversation here.

I bite my lip and open the door beside us, pulling Metjen inside and shutting it before scrambling for the light.

"Taia, I think we're in a cleaning cupboard," he says, so close that his breath tickles my skin.

"I don't care where we are. What's going on?" I ask, finally finding the light and switching it on.

We're closer together than I thought we were, and it's almost impossible to ignore that.

"I don't want to talk about it."

"Stop lying." I mean to say it angrily, but instead, it comes out with a slight squeak and some tears in the corner of my eye. "Please, Metjen, stop lying to me."

He sighs and pushes a hand over his face. "I don't want to have this conversation."

"Well, that one was only half a lie," I mutter. "I guess we're getting somewhere."

"You really want to know?"

"Would I have pulled you into a cupboard after one of the most stressful revelations of our Blessed career if I didn't?" I ask.

"Fair point."

"Why have you been avoiding me?" The moment the question is out in the open, I feel relief. We can deal with this now, even if the answer isn't what I want it to be.

"Is there any point in denying that I have been?" he asks.

"I wouldn't believe you even if I wasn't able to tell when you're lying," I counter.

He sighs. "I was jealous, okay?"

My Blessed sense tingles. "Ani was right," I mutter.

"What? What's Ani got to do with any of this?"

"It's fine, it's just something she said at the banquet the other night. It doesn't matter. What were you jealous of?" I try to quell the hope rising up inside me, but there's nothing I can do about it, not when he's more or less confirmed Ani's theory of what's going on.

"You went on your date with the coffin-maker."

"I did. But I've gone on dates before and you haven't started avoiding me after." Well, two previous dates, but we'll skip over that part.

"I didn't feel this way before."

"Oh." At least now it helps that I can tell he's being truthful.

"I'm sorry."

"I know," I whisper. "So can we stop doing whatever we're doing?"

He nods.

"Really?" I ask.

"I think I have it under control, but I can't promise what will happen when you bring him back to our flat."

I blink a few times. "Are you serious?"

"I can't just switch off the way I'm feeling, Taia."

He raises his hands in frustration, brushing against me as he does.

"Metjen, the date went terribly. I hated every minute of it and came home wanting to tell you all about it."

He blinks a few times. "It did?"

"Of course it did. People hate dating Ma'at Blessed, you know that."

"I mean, I don't have it as bad as you once people realise I can't tell when they're lying," he points out.

"Yeah, so imagine what it's like going on a date and that's *all* someone can think about. It's not fun. I had a bad time and I just wanted my friend, and you weren't there. And somehow, despite the fact we live *and* work together, you've managed to ignore me for days."

A guilty expression crosses his face. "I didn't know how else to deal with what I want."

My mouth goes dry and I worry that I'm interpreting the tone of his voice wrong.

But there's one way to know for sure. "What do you want, Metjen?"

I meet his gaze, seeing the intensity within them and knowing what his answer is going to be even before he says it out loud.

"You, Taia. I want you."

I suck in a deep breath. "Even if it makes us a cliché?"

He chuckles and reaches out to touch my arm. Tingles spread over my skin as he does it.

"We're not a cliché, Taia." His voice comes out hoarser than I expect it to. "I know it feels that way because a lot of the Blessed pairs are together, but it makes sense. We have to trust each other more than anyone else."

"You believe that."

"You know I do," he responds softly.

"It wasn't a question."

"There are other things I believe," he says. "I think that you're smart, beautiful, determined, and loyal."

"Go on."

He raises an eyebrow. "That's not enough for you?"

"I want to hear more about what you think," I respond, stepping closer, not that there's much room left for us to move in the cupboard.

He doesn't push me away, Not that I thought he was going to.

"Let's see, what else can I tell you? The moment you told me that Heqet had set you up on a date, I wanted it to be me."

"Why didn't you say anything?" I ask.

"Because I didn't know how you felt about me."

"Oh."

"I still don't, you haven't actually told me other than being mad at me for ignoring you," he points out.

"Rightly so."

He snorts. "Yeah, okay, fair enough."

"I've been feeling the same," I admit softly. "The jealousy, wishing I was the one you were going on dates with."

"I haven't been on a date in months, Taia."

I nod. "I know."

"So, where does that leave us?" he asks.

I bite my bottom lip and his gaze drops straight there, leaving no doubt in my mind of what he's thinking.

I close the gap further and go up on my toes, pausing when I'm barely an inch away, needing to be sure that this is something he actually wants.

Metjen closes the gap and presses his lips against mine, kissing me deeply.

I sink into him, accepting everything this means. For us, for our duty, and for our future. Neither of us would be going through with this kiss if we thought it was a bad idea.

I just hope we're right about that. And that our goddess doesn't decide that she disapproves.

SIX

DOZENS of nervous Ma'at Blessed fill the room. I doubt any of them have any reason to worry, but I understand exactly what's going through their heads because I'm feeling it too. The huge scales which dominate the front of the room loom above us, impossible to ignore and even more impossible to forget.

I glance at the spot beside me, surprised that Metjen isn't here already. I know he had some kind of appointment this morning, but it's still strange that he's not already here when it's the Scales Test, probably the most important day of our lives as Blessed.

Especially with everything that's changing between us. We still need to talk about some of the things that are changing, and exactly what they're going to mean, particularly for our living arrangements, but this is the chance for us to find out what our goddess thinks of what's growing between us. If she approves or not will show in her blessings.

Or that's the theory. I'm not sure how true it is, or if the older Blessed just imply it's like that so we all behave more and think twice about fooling around with other Blessed.

A hand reaches out to brush against my arm and I jump slightly.

"Just me," Metjen says, sliding into position beside me and straightening his collar over his bare chest.

"You didn't wear a shirt for your formal wear," I say, unsure where it's coming from or why that's what I'm blurting out.

He chuckles. "Is that really what you're thinking about right now?"

"Sorry, it's just that when we were at the street party, I was thinking that I was disappointed that you were wearing a shirt."

"Well that's something I'm going to remember next time I have to wear formal clothing," he jokes. "I guess we should add something else to our list of things to talk about?"

I bite my bottom lip and nod.

"Okay, we can do that," he responds.

"Really? You're not going to try and argue that we're going too fast?"

"After that kiss in the cupboard? Definitely not. We're going to get through this ceremony, and then we're going to go from there," he says.

The High Priestess' voice rings out through the room as she calls the first Blessed Pair to be judged by the scales, starting the test.

"Your circlet is wonky," Metjen whispers, reaching out to straighten it.

"Thanks," I murmur. "I don't know what to expect from any of this."

Metjen shrugs. "It's going to be okay. We'll see at least one honourable discharge today, but other than that, I don't see anyone being let go."

"Wait, someone's going to get fired?"

He nods. "I heard that Ritho asked to leave the temple earlier this year, she wants to start a family with her husband and wants to dedicate her life to that."

My eyes widen. "I don't know if I could do that."

"She probably didn't either until it was on the table," he points out.

He doesn't say it out loud, but I can hear the additional thought in his head. Maybe one day it'll be us making that decision, though there are plenty of Ma'at Blessed who continue to serve even once they've started a family.

A gasp goes through the Blessed surrounding us and my eyes snap to the front in time to see the right side of the scales dip down without a feather in sight.

My eyes widen and I glance at Metjen who shakes his head, clearly as confused as I am.

"Who is it?" the priestess in front of me asks her partner.

"Pasht, I think," she responds. "I didn't realise she wasn't trustworthy."

I glance at Metjen, worry hitting me in another wave. This isn't the dismissal expected, and as a dishonourable one, it's sure to send shockwaves through the temple.

"What happens now?" I ask the two priestesses, unable to help myself.

The one on the left twists so she can see me better. "Every judgement she's made since the last Scales Test will have to be checked by us to ensure that she hasn't compromised on any of them in order to have Ma'at remove her blessing. After that, nothing, I guess."

"Oh." I let that process for a moment.

"What about her Blessed partner?" Metjen asks.

The woman shrugs. "I assume she'll be paired

with someone else. If there's no one here, then probably someone from one of the temples from around the country. There's always a few discharges, nothing to worry about."

"Thanks," I say, trying not to think about what that means for the rest of us.

Metjen brushes a reassuring hand across my back as the next Ma'at Blessed pair approaches the scales. "I know you're worried, but it's going to be fine," he assures me.

"I know. I think," I say back quietly. "But I can't help it."

He nods. "Understandable."

Ritho and her Blessed partner make their way up to the front. Nerves spring to life inside me as I wait for them to approach the shimmering golden scales. Two feathers sit on either side, representing their status as Blessed. Ritho gives her partner a sad but relieved smile as the feather on her side disappears and the scales begin to tip upwards.

An honourable discharge from the Temple of Ma'at. It wasn't something I ever considered to be possible until this moment, and I'm still not entirely sure why I think someone would want it, but it's clear from the expression on her face that this *is* what she wants, and that she doesn't see it as a bad thing. I'm happy for her, even if it's not the outcome I want myself.

She nods her head to the Head Blessed Pair and makes her way out of the room, leaving behind her life in the temple. Perhaps her Blessed partner will find himself paired with Pasht's former partner, but it's a mystery that will have to be left for another day, especially as another pair are called to take their turn.

Metjen reaches out and takes my hand in his, giving it a squeeze. I'm not sure if it's allowed, but the whole ceremony has the feel of both something incredibly formal and not at the same time.

Several more pairs take their turns, all of them staying Blessed, as is to be expected.

"Blessed Priestess Taia and Blessed Priest Metjen," the High Priestess calls.

I exchange a nervous expression with Metjen and head with him towards the head of the room.

I swallow my nerves and try to keep a serene expression on my face, but I'm not sure how well I manage to do that. This is the most nervous I've been since my own Day of Choosing. I don't want Ma'at to take away my blessing, I don't know what I'd do with my life if I didn't work for her.

Metjen catches my eye and gives me a small smile that I assume is him trying to tell me that everything's going to be okay, and I don't have anything to worry about. As much as I want to believe him, there's a part of me that just can't. So much has changed in the past week that I'm worrying about this more than I expected.

It doesn't help that the scales are even more immense when this close to them. They stand higher than any person and look as if they were placed there by a god. Which is probably what the people who built them intended.

Two golden feathers shimmer on either side of the scales, the one on the left for me, the one on the right for Metjen. I stare at my feather, still fearing that it's going to disappear.

A shimmer comes over it, but it stays firmly in place, and the scales remain balanced.

"Ma'at continues to bestow her blessing upon you both," the High Priestess says.

"Thank you," I murmur, dipping my head to the head of the temple, and then to the scales in turn. I have no idea if they are Ma'at personified, but they're the conduit of her power in this moment, and that's enough for me.

I turn around and start to head back to my place. Metjen reaches out and catches my hand in his, entwining our fingers together. I relax into his touch, relieved that we've passed the test I was so worried about.

"We did it," he whispers to me as we take our place in the line-up of priests.

"We did," I say with relief, resisting the urge to lay my head on his shoulder when there are so many people around.

"I have a question for you," he says.

"Mmm?"

"Would you like to go on a date with me?"

My heart skips a beat. "I'm free later."

"We have a banquet to attend."

I groan.

"You could be my date to the banquet," he jokes.

"You're already my date to the banquet, you're my Blessed partner and it's the end of the Festival banquet," I point out.

"Ah, funny how that worked out."

I snort. "Fine, but then you're going to owe me a midnight snack. You know I get hungry after these things."

"Consider it sorted." The way he smiles at me makes me certain that this is going to be the start of something special. And with Ma'at not removing either of our blessings, it seems that even our goddess approves.

SEVEN

I MAKE my way through the market, checking to make sure I'm going in the right direction for the tea stand that Ani messaged me about. I've never been before, but from what she's said, she and Nik come to the food stands here all the time when they want to get out of their temple.

I spot the sign, surprised to find that it's more than just a stand and is actually a small building. At least that means there's going to be somewhere to sit.

Ani turns and spots me approaching, waving me over enthusiastically. I make my way over, only pausing when I notice that Nik is with her, something I didn't expect.

"Hey, Taia," she says brightly. "Don't mind him,

he's just leaving." She touches his arm affectionately.

Nik chuckles. "Nice to know you want rid of me."

"Yes, that's it. Nothing to do with your meeting," she responds.

He leans in and kisses her cheek. "I'll tell you all about it later."

"You'd better."

He waves and heads out of the stand.

"Should we grab a table?" Ani asks.

I nod.

Matia starts whining from beside her.

"Oh shhh," the Anubis Blessed says. "You'll see him again soon."

I look at the jackal, somewhat confused by her reaction. "Is she okay?"

"She's fine, she's just whining cause Nik's leaving her. I swear she loves him more than she loves me sometimes." She takes a seat at the table in the corner and I go to join her.

"I don't think that's normal." At least, I've never heard any of the other Blessed animals acting like that.

Ani shrugs and scratches the jackal's head affectionately. "I think she's just used to him being around. You should see her trying to make sure she can cuddle him in bed. No, sorry, that's a weird thing to say."

I let out a small laugh. "It's fine, it's not like I don't know you're together or anything."

She nods and looks down at the table. "Yeah, I guess that's not going to be a secret from anyone much longer."

"I think everyone already knows. It's one of the worst-kept secrets in London," I say affectionately. "I knew about the two of you before we even met."

"We've never really done much to hide it," she admits. "But it'll be different soon. We're getting married. Wow, that's weird to tell someone. I'm going to have to get used to that."

"Congratulations, that's good, right?"

A soft smile crosses her face. "There's nothing I want more."

My Blessed sense tingles, though I'm not surprised. No one who has seen the way the two of them look at one another can deny that.

"Then I'm happy for you," I say.

"Thanks, but we're not here to talk about that, you promised you'd tell me what happened with Metjen."

I chuckle. "I'm pretty sure friends are supposed to talk about all kinds of things, not just one."

A server arrives with a pot of tea and two cups, setting it down between us without another word.

I raise an eyebrow. "Aren't we supposed to order?"

"They only do one thing here," Ani responds. "But they do it well." She picks up the pot and pours for both of us.

"Oh."

"So, Metjen?" she prompts.

"Things are good, I think. It's really early, but we talked about it, and you were completely right about the jealousy thing. It turns out that we were both developing feelings towards each other but neither of us was brave enough to tell the other."

"Isn't that something you'd be able to tell with your Blessed sense?" she asks.

I shake my head. "If I'd asked him outright if he wanted more, I'd have known if he was lying to me. But other than that, it's actually pretty useless."

"Ah, so if I ask a question, your Blessed sense doesn't respond?"

"Not unless your question was also a truth. So I know how you feel about your upcoming marriage, but I don't know how you feel about the fact Matia apparently likes Nik so much, for example. You've never told me anything about it, so I don't know the truth." I wrap my hands around the teacup and take a sip, letting out a loud sigh. "Okay, that's good."

"It is," she agrees. "And if you want to know, the answer is that I love it."

My Blessed sense tingles.

"I think seeing the way he was with her was one of the ways I knew I loved him," she explains. "She's such an important part of me and who I am, and he never makes me feel as if she's an afterthought, or in the way. She's just part of our unit."

I nod.

"So, how did I do?" Ani asks, a genuinely curious note in her voice.

"You can't tell?" I ask.

She shrugs. "I know how I think I feel, I guess that doesn't mean I *do* feel that way."

"Ah. Well, you believe everything you've told me."

"Good." She sits back in her seat with a happy smile on her face. Matia rests her head on Ani's knee, and the other Blessed starts stroking her. "So what's next with you and Metjen?"

"I guess normal relationship stuff. I honestly don't have much experience. And most of my friends from school have already fallen out of touch. Being Ma'at Blessed is..." I trail off, not knowing who is listening.

"Hard?" Ani finishes for me.

"Yeah. And it can be lonely," I admit quietly. "I guess that was one of the reasons I was worried about what would happen if I told Metjen how I felt. Being a Ma'at Blessed while your partner is being weird with you is bad."

"Can you not change partners?"

I shake my head. "There's only one way to break a Ma'at Blessed pair."

"By undoing the blessing?" she guesses.

"Yeah. It happens." I think back to the Scales Test and repress a shiver. "Not that often."

"Interesting. I always worry that I'm going to do something that will make Anubis remove his blessing." The words are barely audible, but I hear them, and the truth within them.

"I doubt that will happen while you're worrying about it," I point out. "And considering everything you've done for your temple already."

"Don't you ever worry about it?" she asks.

"I worried about it last week," I admit. "Part of the Festival of the Blessed was a test for us."

Surprise flits across Ani's face, which I assume must mean that they don't do the same in the Temple of Anubis. Which isn't a huge surprise. Anubis doesn't bless many people, and she was the first to be Blessed in London in a long time.

"I wasn't just worried about Metjen not speaking to me for personal reasons, but because of the test too. I was worried that it would count against us and that Ma'at would remove her blessing."

"Oh, Taia, I'm so sorry. And I'm even more sorry that you didn't have anyone to talk to about it."

I can feel the truth in her words and it gives me a reassured feeling that I'm grateful for. "I guess that can change now?"

"It can." She smiles at me in a way that makes me feel like I've judged her right.

Then again, it's hard to judge someone wrong when you can tell if they're telling the truth. I wouldn't need that with Ani, though. What she and Nik did with getting my temple involved in the corruption in theirs was really brave. I'm not entirely sure I'd have been able to do it in their position and I literally work for the goddess of justice. But it tells me a lot about the kind of people they both are.

"It's fine, we passed anyway, there's nothing to worry about for another five years," I say.

She sighs. "And then there'll be another Festival, and we'll have to do last week all over again."

"You sound the way I feel about it."

"It was a hard week. I'm not sure if it'll be any

easier in five years' time, even if there's a chance I'll have another Blessed with me."

"It's got to get easier as time goes on, right?" I say. "The others seemed to be enjoying themselves."

"Hmm. True." She takes a sip of her tea. "And it'll be better to be able to go back to a house I share with just Nik after being exhausted, rather than having to deal with our flatmates. Don't get me wrong, I love Hannu and Ibi to bits, but they aren't easy to live with."

I chuckle. "I hear you, living with Metjen hasn't been the easiest. I've barely dated in the past three years, and I'm pretty sure that's the reason why."

She raises an eyebrow. "Because of the morning after?"

I nod. "Can you imagine? He'd know exactly what I'd been doing, and that's just...no."

She lets out a light-hearted laugh. "Yeah, that took some getting used to. But we all got used to it after a bit."

"The only problem is that now I'm really out of touch," I admit. "It's a while since I've...I'm sorry, you don't need to hear this."

"Do you have anyone else you can talk to about it?"

I think for a moment, trying to consider whether there's anyone at the temple. "Only Metjen, I guess."

"Okay, then now you have me. What's on your mind?"

I study her intently.

"What? It's a genuine offer," she responds.

"I know. I think you just confuse me," I say.

She shrugs. "It's not intentional."

"I know that too."

"Hmm, this could get old fast," she jokes.

"Think how it feels on this end," I mutter. "If someone lies to me, then I know it. Which is fine for big stuff, really useful when buying jewels, but it's not great when someone is lying about something like telling you that you look good."

"Has anyone ever done that?" she asks curiously.

I wrinkle my nose. "My grandmother. I wouldn't have needed my Blessed sense to know that she wasn't telling me the truth, but it was still there to point a shining beacon on the lie."

"What about when Metjen tells you about how you look?"

"He's telling the truth. Always."

"Not a surprise." She takes a sip of her tea.

"I guess not."

"Okay, so what haven't you done in a while that's got you worried?" Ani asks.

"I think the shorter answer is what *have* I done.

I've been on three dates since I was Blessed, and only one of them ended in a kiss."

"Ah, I see."

"You do?"

She nods. "You're worried about all the stuff that comes after the kiss."

"Pretty much."

"I did too, a bit," she says. "And it took us a while until we were ready for that. But if you're there already, I have a friend at Bastet's temple who can help you out."

"You do?"

She nods. "We went to school together, so I know for sure she's trustworthy. I can ask her to make you an appointment if you want?"

"I'd like that. If you think that's okay and she won't find it weird."

"Trust me, it'll be weird." She gives a small uncomfortable laugh. "When I went to get all that stuff sorted, I was doing everything possible to avoid her, only to end up with her being the one who was doing the contraception consultations that day. Talk about irony. But she's really good at her job, she'll be able to help."

"Thank you, Ani, I appreciate it."

"Hey, I don't even need your Blessed sense to be

able to tell that you're telling the truth there," she jokes.

Interestingly, my Blessed sense responds like she's telling the truth.

"Metjen says I'm easy to read too," I say.

"Maybe for him, but I can't get anything out of you most of the time, I just happened to then. It'll probably change as we get to know each other better." She pulls out her phone and taps a few buttons. "There you go, I sent you her info. I'll let her know to expect you too."

"Thanks."

"And if you want company, let me know. I'll come with you."

"Won't that be extra awkward?"

She shrugs. "Probably. But what are friends for?"

The way she says it is so matter-of-fact that it tells me exactly how she thinks about the current situation. And I like it. I need a friend who understands it all, the Blessed complications and the normal ones, and even if Ani's blessing is from another god, it means that she understands me in a way that other people can't. I might have lost the friends I had from before I joined the Temple of Ma'at, but at least now I have a chance to make new ones.

EIGHT

I PAUSE outside our front door, not knowing what to expect when I get inside. Things seem to have been going well with Metjen, but we've been so busy with work that we haven't had much time to properly explore whatever this is between us.

But now we have a full evening ahead of us and a day off tomorrow.

I push open the door and stop in my tracks as I take in the sight of our living area. The table is pushed out of the way and a blanket covers the floor, laden with what looks like all of our favourite foods.

"What did you do?" I ask.

"What does it look like?" Metjen asks, coming to greet me with a glass of what looks like cherry wine. He hands it to me and kisses my cheek.

"It looks like you've prepared a feast."

"Technically, I went to the market and bought the feast, I didn't do any prep." He steers me towards the blanket and gestures for me to sit down.

I lean back against our sofa and take a sip of wine. Metjen comes to join me, sitting so close that our legs touch.

"How was your meeting with Ani? You seem to have a lot of those this week. Is everything all right over at their temple?"

A fierce blush flares over my cheeks. "I wasn't at her temple," I admit.

"Oh?"

I take another sip of wine while I try to work out the best way to broach the subject. "So you know how I've been struggling with the not having friends thing."

"Mmm."

"Well, Ani promised she'd help me with some things that friends would normally do."

"You're being very cryptic," Metjen responds, picking up an apple and starting to eat it while he listens to me. I'm not sure whether his relaxed attitude makes me feel more at ease, or less.

"She has a friend at the Temple of Bastet and she went with me today to go and have a conversation about..." I trail off.

"About?"

I sigh. "The things that you'd normally go to see a fertility goddess' priestess for."

"Ah. I see. I hadn't realised that you didn't already have things like that in place," he admits.

I groan. "Can we not talk about this?"

"You're the one who went to see a fertility temple," he jokes. "But no, we don't have to if you don't want to."

"It's not that I don't want to." I look down at my lap. "I'm just very out of practice with all of this."

"You're not the only one. But it's okay, it's not like either of us is going anywhere. We can take it slow and at a pace that suits us."

"Are you sure?" The question is needless, I know he's telling the truth, and not just from my Blessed sense, but from the way he's looking at me too.

Warmth fills his gaze. "Yes." He knows he doesn't need to answer, but he does anyway, only making me more comfortable in the situation.

I sigh and lean my head against his shoulder. "This is nice, by the way."

"Even if it's nothing we haven't done before?" I take another sip of my wine and place the glass on the ground by us.

"It's different," he responds.

"How?"

"Because now, instead of *thinking* about kissing you, I can just do this." He leans in and cups my cheek in his hand, his gaze searching my face for the permission he surely already knows is there.

I close the distance between us and press my lips against his. I rest my hand on his chest, feeling the rapid beating of his heart. If his words hadn't already given away precisely how he felt about the whole situation, this certainly would. He's clearly as interested in exploring what this is with me as I am with him.

We break apart and a wide smile spreads across my face, one that's echoed on Metjen's.

"We can do this," I say.

He nods. "We can."

"And Ma'at approves."

"She seems to," he agrees. "I suppose we'll find out for sure in five years."

I chuckle. "Do you really think she'd wait to show her displeasure? This is Ma'at we're talking about."

"She's the goddess of..." he trails off. "Yep, okay, I see your point."

"Fair, but firm and unyielding," I say. "That's what I always liked about her, even as a kid. Ma'at can be predicted if you know what the truth of a matter is. It's the order of things and the way that they're meant to be."

"No wonder you were Blessed," he teases.

"You were too, you can't say that you don't value the same things, clearly Ma'at thinks that you do."

"Is that how the blessings work?"

"I don't know," I admit. "The only person I've talked to about it is Ani."

"And? What do you reckon about why she got her blessing?"

"I guess it's hard to say," I respond. "But I can see why she's Blessed. She says she always wanted to be an embalmer, but it's more than that. She was determined to fix the issues with the temple, even if it made her life harder temporarily."

"Nik did that too, he isn't Blessed."

"Mmm."

"Okay, so you have thoughts on that." He picks up the bottle of wine and holds it out to me. I grab my glass and hold it out to him so he can fill it.

"They're not complete thoughts," I admit. "Have you ever noticed how Matia acts around him?"

"I honestly haven't spent enough time around them all to notice much." He shrugs.

"Right, that would make it hard," I agree. "I've never noticed any of the other Blessed animals acting the way Matia does around Nik. It's weird."

"Almost as if he's Blessed himself?"

I shake my head. "No, Ani says he doesn't have the Blessed sense. It's probably nothing. But I don't want to spend our whole evening talking about other people." I take a sip of wine. "This is good by the way."

"It should be, I got it from the wine vendor you like," he responds.

"Thank you, that's very sweet." I lean in and kiss his cheek.

"I have some making up to do after the whole jealousy thing."

"No, you don't," I assure him. "I get it, the feelings were weird. Maybe it wasn't the best way to deal with it, but for all we know, I might have acted the same way."

"No, I don't think you would have done."

"You clearly have more faith in me than I do. Don't forget I'm capable of lying to you, that's not where your talents lie."

He chuckles. "You *think* you're capable of lying to me. But you forget that we live like this because the temple wants us to know one another inside out. I can tell when you're lying to me, even if you don't say a word."

"Oh, well now I need to test this." I close my

eyes and try to think of a good lie, something that he doesn't already know about me.

"All right, try me."

"I'm going to tell you two truths and a lie," I say. "Then you have to tell me which is the lie."

"Okay." The bemused smile on his face says it all, but I'm determined to prove I'm capable of lying. Which I think is a weird thing to do considering my position here, but it's a fun task to see if he can tell.

"All right, so when I was five, I had a cat and I called him Buttons..."

"Try again, I know your childhood cat was called Sekky. I'm surprised you didn't get punished by Sekhmet for that one."

"I was five. She may be the goddess of vengeance, but she's not heartless."

"Have you seen the way those lions look at us?" A shiver runs down his spine. "Anyway, try again."

"Hmm, okay. Let's see...the first time I saw one of Ma'at's priestesses, I was seven and one of them was visiting our neighbour. I don't know what for, but I remember how powerful she looked. My second statement is that I once swallowed a bee and thought that Ra was punishing me for cursing his name. And my third is that I thought you were really annoying when we first met."

"Hmmm, let's see. I think it's got to be the last one that's the lie."

Triumph fills me. "Aha, it's not! You were super annoying."

A smug smile crosses his face.

"Oh no, what?"

"I knew the second one was the lie."

My Blessed sense tingles. I narrow my eyes at him. "How?"

"Because I know you. And whenever you lie, you wrinkle your nose."

"Eurgh, why didn't you tell me that before?" I ask.

"Because I wanted to see what you came up with," he responds. "So you really thought that I was annoying when we first met?"

"Yes, you had all the righteousness and none of the humility."

He raises an eyebrow. "And you didn't?"

"I never said I wasn't annoying too," I point out. "Just that you were."

"Ah, fair. Well, luckily for both of us, I think we're doing a great job at growing together."

"I think so. We make each other better," I say.

"We're a Blessed Pair, that's exactly what we're supposed to do," Metjen points out. "And there's no one I'd rather do it with."

"Me neither." Being Blessed is as much a burden as it is a gift, but working together, we can make it truly mean something.

THANK you for reading *Scales Of Honesty*, I hope you enjoyed it! If you'd like to learn more about Ani, Nik, and Matia the jackal, you can in *The Apprentice Of Anubis* series, starting with *Apprentice Of The Dead*: https://books2read.com/apprenticeofthedead

AUTHOR NOTE

Thank you for reading *Scales Of Honesty*, I hope you enjoyed it!

I've been considering writing a story for Taia and Metjen ever since they were introduced into the series, but the time has never quite felt right for them until now. When writing Festival Of The Blessed, it finally clicked into place. This is the only time I plan for them to be main characters, but I do plan for them to continue to turn up in Ani and Nik's series, and I do have plans for them to appear in the future series I have planned based in the Temple of Ma'at.

It was interesting to see Ani and Nik (and Matia) from the outside, especially from someone who didn't know Ani before she became Blessed, so that made her appearances very fun to write, especially with some of Taia's observations about what's going on with Nik and Matia! If you haven't started Ani's story, you can find out more about her, Nik, and her sacred jackal in *The Apprentice Of Anubis* series, starting with *Apprentice Of The Dead*.

If you want to keep up to date with new releases and other news, you can join my Facebook Reader Group or mailing list.

Stay safe & happy reading!

- Laura

You can find out more about each of my series on my website.

Obscure Academy

A paranormal romance series set at a university-age academy for mixed supernaturals. Each book follows a different couple.

The Apprentice Of Anubis

An urban fantasy series set in an alternative world where the Ancient Egyptian Empire never fell. It follows a new apprentice to the temple of Anubis as she learns about her new role.

Cauldron Coffee Shop

An urban fantasy series following a witch who discovers a cursed warlock living in a teapot.

The Shifter Season

A paranormal Regency romance series following shifters as they attempt to find their match. Each book follows a different couple.

Forgotten Gods

A paranormal adventure romance series inspired by Egyptian mythology. Each book follows a different Ancient Egyptian goddess.

Amethyst's Wand Shop Mysteries (with Arizona Tape)

An urban fantasy murder mystery series following a witch who teams up with a detective to solve murders. Each book includes a different murder.

Grimm Academy

A fantasy fairy tale academy series. Each book follows a different fairy tale heroine.

Purple Oasis (with Arizona Tape)

A paranormal romance series based at a sanctuary set up after the apocalypse. Each book follows a different couple.

Supernatural Snow Fair

A paranormal romance series based at a Christmas/winter fair. Each book follows a different couple.

Speed Dating With The Denizens Of The Underworld (shared world)

A paranormal romance shared world based on

mythology from around the world. Each book follows a different couple.

Broomstick Bakery

A complete paranormal romance series following a family of witches who run a magical bakery. Each book follows a different couple.

Grimalkin Academy

A complete urban fantasy academy series following a witch cursed to create kittens every time she does magic.

The Paranormal Council

A complete paranormal romance series following paranormals trying to find their fated mates. Each book follows a different couple.

You can find a complete list of all my books on my website:

https://www.authorlauragreenwood.co.uk/p/book-list.html

Signed Paperback & Merchandise:

You can find signed paperbacks, hardcovers, and merchandise based on my series (including stickers, magnets, face masks, and more!) via my website: https://www.authorlauragreenwood.co.uk/p/shop.html

ABOUT LAURA GREENWOOD

Laura is a USA Today Bestselling Author of paranormal, fantasy, urban fantasy, and contemporary romance. When she's not writing, she drinks a lot of tea, tries to resist French macarons, and works towards a diploma in Egyptology. She lives in the UK, where most of her books are set. Laura specialises in quick reads, whether you're looking for a swoonworthy romance for the bath, or an action-packed adventure for your latest journey, you'll find the perfect match amongst her books!

Follow Laura Greenwood

- Website: www.authorlauragreenwood. co.uk
- Mailing List: https://www. authorlauragreenwood.co.uk/p/book-sign-up.html
- Facebook Group: http://facebook.com/ groups/theparanormalcouncil

- Facebook Page: http://facebook.com/authorlauragreenwood
- Bookbub: www.bookbub.com/authors/laura-greenwood